Three River Junction

A Story of an Alaskan Bald Eagle Preserve

To Mom, Dad, and Cara. — S.B.

Dedicated to my children, for it's
their generation we hand the responsibility
of caretakers of God's creatures to. — T.A.

Illustrations copyright © 1997 Tom Antonishak.
Book copyright © 1997 Trudy Corporation, 353 Main Avenue, Norwalk, CT 06851.

Soundprints is a division of Trudy Corporation, Norwalk, Connecticut.

Book Design: Shields & Partners, Westport, CT

First Edition 1997
10 9 8 7 6 5 4 3
Printed in China

Acknowledgments:
   Our very special thanks to Bill Zack, Haines Chief Ranger, Alaska State Parks,
for his review and guidance.

Library of Congress Cataloging-in-Publication Data

Burnham, Saranne D.

Three river junction : a story of an Alaskan bald eagle preserve /
by Saranne D. Burnham ; illustrated by Tom Antonishak.
        p.   cm.
Summary: After arriving at an Alaskan preserve, a hungry bald eagle searches
for food and interacts with the other eagles there.
        ISBN 1-56899-441-9(hardcover)   ISBN 1-56899-422-7 (pbk.)
1. Bald eagle — Juvenile fiction. [1. Bald eagle — Fiction.   2. Eagles — Fiction.
3. Alaska—Fiction.] I. Antonishak, Tom, ill. II. Title.
        PZ10.3.B9353Th 1997   96-39090
        [E] — dc21   CIP
                                                                         AC

Three River Junction

A Story of an Alaskan Bald Eagle Preserve

by Saranne D. Burnham
Illustrated by Tom Antonishak

Soundprints™
Where Children Discover...

All that can be heard above the vast blanket of trees is the creaking and snapping of frozen hemlocks and the soft lapping of water against the gravel shore. The late November sun seems small and distant; the air is cold and bitter.

As the strengthening wind blows, a lone bald eagle catches a gust and soars effortlessly through the air. He passes over the Klukwan native village and dips down toward the junction, where the Tsirku and Kleheni rivers pour into the great Chilkat. Mist rises off the water. The air begins to clear.

The eagle glides swiftly over the rivers and lakes that split up the snow speckled landscape beneath him. The seven-foot span of his wings sends a speeding shadow across the treetops. More than a week ago he left his autumn home, where the rivers were beginning to freeze and food was growing scarce.

Now, he soars above the Chilkat Bald Eagle Preserve in southeast Alaska. Here, warm water flowing from an underground reservoir keeps the river from freezing during the cold winter months.

The eagle circles, surveying the area.

7

Below, the preserve is full of activity as wildlife in the forest ready their shelter and food supply for the long winter ahead. It will be a busy day on the banks of the Chilkat River.

Slipping and rolling, a river otter slides into the clear water in search of his morning meal. Two seagulls squawk and fight over a dying salmon that floats near the water's surface. They are fearless of the coming winter. The spawned-out fish are an easy catch, and there are plenty to go around.

Quickly but carefully, a red squirrel buries a mouthful of seeds beneath a frost-wilted fern at the trunk of a fallen spruce. In the cold winter months this hidden feast will come in handy.

Surrounding the fallen tree are the scattered remains of the eagle's giant nest. The nest has lain here since a summer storm brought down the tall spruce. Next spring, when the eagle is ready to raise eaglets, he will have to build another.

For now, the twigs and leaves that made up the six-foot nest are perfect materials for the squirrel to use to strengthen his home. He stuffs his cheeks with dry leaves and scurries up the hundred-foot trunk of a hemlock, where his nest is waiting.

The activity of the forest does not escape the eagle's notice. He is hungry after his long journey. From high in the air, his sharp eyes catch the movement of a snowshoe hare, white against the snow below. He streaks toward it, claws out front, ready.

Nibbling a willow, the snowshoe hare sees a blur of movement as the eagle plummets toward it. The snowshoe hare darts for the shelter of a nearby alder, but it is too far.

Just as the eagle's sharp talons are ready to grab the snowshoe hare, it changes direction in mid-air. With three long leaps it dives into the safety of its hidden burrow.

Still hungry, the eagle comes to rest on a cottonwood snag. Over two hundred feet straight down the rough, brown trunk of the tree, the Chilkat River runs idly by.

A moose wades chest deep through the river's current. Magpies hop on the gravel shore, searching for scraps of food dropped by the squabbling seagulls. Nearby, the otter relaxes on a log, full from a breakfast of salmon.

Then, from over the treetops, another bald eagle arrives in the preserve.

The first eagle watches as the newcomer glides toward the water in search of prey.

Seeing slow moving salmon, the newcomer lands on the shore. He carefully wades into the shallows of the icy cold river, to where the spawned-out salmon swirl in the shade of the cottonwoods. He approaches them and swiftly snatches one in his sharp beak. The newcomer secures his wriggling catch in his talons and takes off down the river.

The bald eagle sees the newcomer's success and rockets toward him, screaming and calling.

He shoots across the treetops and down along the river. Closing in on the other eagle from below, he suddenly flips over and flies on his back with talons up. In an instant, he rips the salmon from the newcomer's grasp.

Triumphant, the eagle rights himself and continues down over the Chilkat River. He lands on a beach to eat his catch. The beat of his giant wings causes a flurry of activity as seagulls and magpies jump out of his way. They watch from a safe distance, in case there are leftovers.

Holding the dying salmon down with his finger-like claws, the eagle enjoys his stolen meal. Then, he takes flight, leaving the carcass on the beach for the magpies.

His hunger satisfied, the eagle heads upriver
again toward the perch in the cottonwood snag.
But as he approaches, he sees that a golden eagle,
a rare visitor to the preserve, has settled there.
The bald eagle lets out a piercing shriek, scaring
the intruder away.

As the pale November sun creeps across the horizon, the eagle roosts in the uppermost branches of the snag. Other bald eagles perch around him, surveying the abundant river valley. Below, the otter makes a slide in fresh snow, and in the shallows of the river, the moose sips from the waters.

All afternoon the eagles stand tall and still, ever watchful atop the vast forest.

The short Alaskan day soon draws to a close. As the sun sinks behind the trees, the squirrel curls into his nest. The otter slinks into his lodge in a protected bend in the river, and the moose disappears into the forest.

Evening falls and the temperature drops, a bitter reminder of the months to come. On the riverbank, the cottonwoods turn white with new-fallen snow. The eagle settles with the others in a cottonwood beneath the shelter of the forest canopy, preserving energy through the long Alaskan night.

Chilkat Bald Eagle Preserve

Bald Eagles can be found in the Chilkat Bald Eagle Preserve in southeastern Alaska. Every winter, 4,000 eagles come to the preserve — that's the largest gathering of bald eagles in the world.

About the Alaska Chilkat Bald Eagle Preserve

Located in southeast Alaska, the Chilkat Bald Eagle Preserve is an Alaska State Park unit set aside to protect the bald eagles that gather there each winter. The preserve, as well as the river that flows through it, is named for the Chilkat people, a tribe of Native Americans that has lived on the land and revered the bald eagle for hundreds of years. Today many of the Chilkat people live on the border of the preserve, which they call "The Council Grounds."

Three rivers flow through the Chilkat Preserve, the Chilkat, Kleheni, and Tsirku. In the fall, salmon lay their eggs, or "spawn," in these rivers. After spawning, the salmon begin to die. The spawned-out salmon are perfect food for the eagles. And while most of the rivers and streams in Alaska begin to freeze in the fall, making it impossible for the eagles to catch salmon, warm water from an underground reservoir keeps the Chilkat River flowing and allows the eagles to eat in the fall and early winter.

Up to 4,000 bald eagles come to the preserve to fish for salmon during the cold winter months. By protecting the area, people ensure that the bald eagle, once an endangered species, can continue to live in the wild.

Glossary

 *Golden Eagle*

 *Red Squirrel*

 *Magpie*

 *Snowshoe Hare*

 *Otter*

 *Timberwolf*

Bald Eagle

Sea Gull

Moose

Bald Eagle Carrying Spawned-out Salmon